SuperBook®
THE FIERY FURNACE!

Most Charisma House Book Group products are available at special quantity discounts for bulk purchase for sales promotions, premiums, fund-raising, and educational needs. For details, call us at (407) 333-0600 or visit our website at charismahouse.com.

Story adapted by Jason Richards and published by Charisma House, 600 Rinehart Road, Lake Mary, Florida 32746

International Standard Book Number: 978-1-62999-969-2

21 22 23 24 25 — 987654321

Printed in China

Chris Quantum ran out of his room, yelling for his robot. "Gizmo, I'm late for school!" His hair was a mess, and he couldn't find his books.

As Gizmo tried to help Chris, his classmates Mitch and Jay called. "Did you study?"

Chris gasped. "No. For what?"

"The science test!" said Jay. "If you don't pass, you can't take the class trip to the amusement park and ride the new roller coaster!"

"I've got to ride it!" Chris moaned. "But how can I pass the test?"

"Well, we have all the answers if you want to buy them," Mitch announced. "I'll send you the link." And he hung up.

For a moment, Chris wondered what to do. Then he thought about that new roller coaster—and he clicked on the link to buy the test answers.

Gizmo pleaded, "Don't do it!"

"It's fine," said Chris. "Just don't tell Joy."

But guess who had stopped by on the way to school? Their friend Joy Pepper. She warned, "Chris Quantum, that's cheating!"

Suddenly, Chris, Joy, and Gizmo found themselves swept up into a swirling vortex.

"It's Superbook!" they shouted.

"I am taking you to meet three men who chose to obey God despite terrible danger," Superbook declared.

And away they went to Babylon, going far back in time—about five hundred years before Christ was born!

They landed in an empty house, but it wasn't empty for long! Three men walked in. "Oh," said one with a smile, "we have guests!"

Joy introduced herself, along with Chris and Gizmo, adding, "We're not from around here."

The first man nodded. "We are not from here either. I am Shadrach, and these are my friends Meshach and Abednego. We are Jews from Jerusalem who were taken captive to serve the king of Babylon."

"We miss our homeland," added Meshach, "but we've been given good jobs here. Things have gone pretty well for us— until now!"

Abednego pointed out the window to a huge statue made of gold. He said, "King Nebuchadnezzar has ordered everyone to bow down to his statue and worship it."

"What's the problem?" asked Chris.

"Our God is the one true God, and He commands us not to

worship any other gods," Shadrach explained. "But the king says that anyone who does not bow down to the statue will be thrown into a blazing furnace!"

"Yikes!" Joy blurted out.

Soon it was time for the people to gather in front of the king's gigantic golden statue.

An official loudly proclaimed, "When you hear the musical instruments play, you must bow to the ground and worship the statue!"

Chris, Joy, and Gizmo watched from a distance as their new friends faced a terrible decision. Would Shadrach, Meshach, and Abednego disobey God and bow down—or would they risk their lives by standing up?

Suddenly, the music began to play—horns, flutes, pipes, stringed instruments, and more. Like a wave sweeping across the ocean, the people in the crowd began to bow.

Everyone was on their knees with their faces to the ground—everyone, that is, except Shadrach, Meshach, and Abednego. They were standing tall!

The king was furious! "I'll give you one more chance to serve my gods and worship the statue," he roared. "But if you don't, no god can save you!"

Bravely, the three men refused. "Our God is able to save us," they said. "But even if He doesn't, we will never serve your

gods or worship the statue."

The king looked as if he might explode! He screamed, "Then heat the furnace seven times hotter!"

Chris, Joy, and Gizmo had to turn away. They could not bear to watch the guards throw Shadrach, Meshach, and Abednego into the flames.

"They can't possibly live through that," whispered Chris. Now he understood how courageous the men were. They had chosen to obey God, no matter what happened.

But then they heard the king ask, "Didn't we tie up *three* men and throw them into the fire?" He rubbed his eyes. "I see *four* men, untied, walking around unharmed! And the fourth man looks like a god!"

Joy peeked at the furnace. "Who is that in there with them?" she wondered.

Chris could hardly believe what he saw. "It must be...God!"

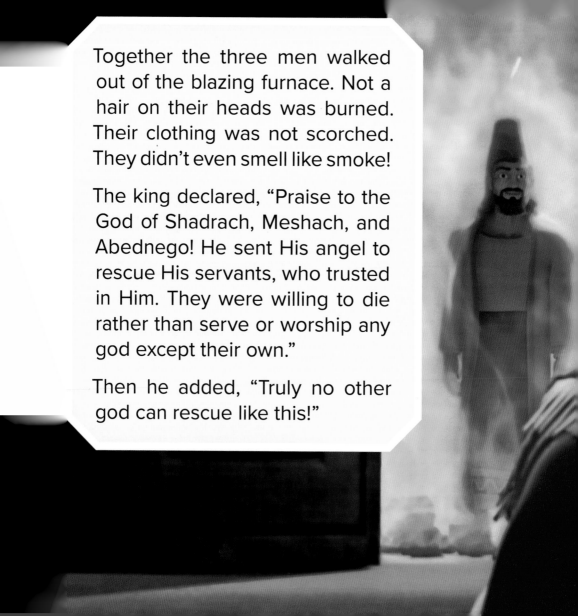

Together the three men walked out of the blazing furnace. Not a hair on their heads was burned. Their clothing was not scorched. They didn't even smell like smoke!

The king declared, "Praise to the God of Shadrach, Meshach, and Abednego! He sent His angel to rescue His servants, who trusted in Him. They were willing to die rather than serve or worship any god except their own."

Then he added, "Truly no other god can rescue like this!"

The king also gave Shadrach, Meshach, and Abednego more-important jobs than they'd had before.

As Chris walked out of the palace with Joy and Gizmo, he thought about how much the three men had been blessed for obeying God. Suddenly, there was a blinding flash of light. Superbook was taking them back home!

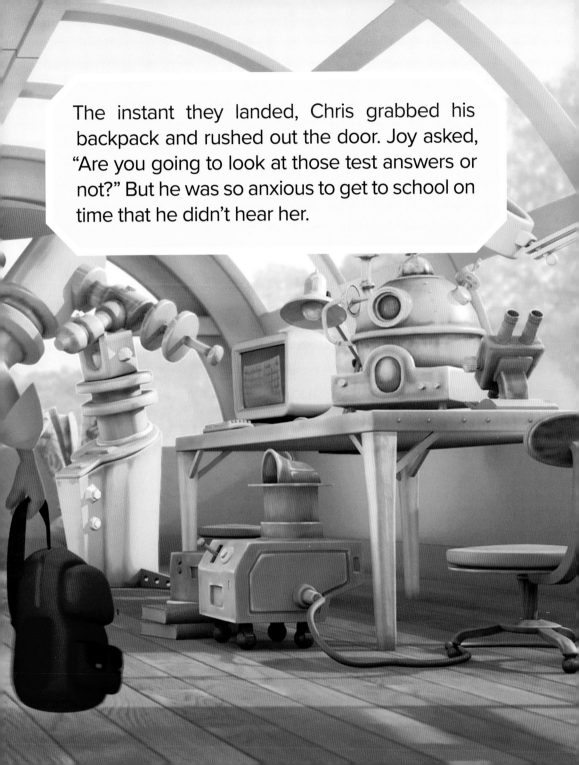

The instant they landed, Chris grabbed his backpack and rushed out the door. Joy asked, "Are you going to look at those test answers or not?" But he was so anxious to get to school on time that he didn't hear her.

The next day, Chris was disappointed to see his test grade. The teacher stopped him in the hallway and said, "Chris, a lot of kids cheated by using the answers from last year's exam. They all failed." Chris looked at the floor, feeling awkward. She continued, "I hear that you also had the answers but decided not to look at them."

Chris lowered his head sadly. "Yes, I took the test on my own—but I know I didn't do quite well enough to go to the amusement park."

"You didn't cheat," his teacher replied. "That deserves some credit." Then she added with a smile, "Have fun at the park!"

Chris looked up in surprise. "Wow, thanks!" he exclaimed. And as he pictured himself riding the new roller coaster, he was really glad that he had made the right choice!

"God blesses those who patiently endure testing and temptation."

—James 1:12